This is an old story. The author used to tell it as bedtime stories to his children. It was always about a plucky rabbit, Hoppity-Hop, who fought naughty beasts defending his friends, the good animals of the forest. The stories were in prose and never written. Then came the grandchildren and as a joking Swedish saying goes, "if I knew that the grandchildren are so sweet, I had conceived them before my children". So the stories were written in verse, the result being the present book.

Anton

AuthorHouse™ UK
1663 Liberty Drive
Bloomington, IN 47403 USA
www.authorhouse.co.uk
Phone: 0800 047 8203 (Domestic TFN)
+44 1908 723714 (International)

Because of the dynamic nature of the Internet, any web addresses or links contained in this
book may have changed since publication and may no longer be valid. The views expressed
in this work are solely those of the author and do not necessarily reflect the views of
the publisher, and the publisher hereby disclaims any responsibility for them.

Any people depicted in stock imagery provided by Getty Images are models,
and such images are being used for illustrative purposes only.
Certain stock imagery © Getty Images.

This book is printed on acid-free paper.

ISBN: 978-1-7283-9966-9 (sc)
978-1-7283-9965-2 (e)

Print information available on the last page.

Published by AuthorHouse 03/10/2020

authorHOUSE

Anton Sanda

The Amazing Adventures of Hoppity-Hop the Rabbit

Illustrations by:
Catalin Nedelcu

In a land as in dreams fair,
With none other to compare,
And as stunning as in tales,
Where true beauty still prevails,
With green mountains capped with snow,
Rivers crossing down below,
There lived on a hilltop
A plucky rabbit, Hoppity-Hop.

He was so unafraid and brave,
Always keen to go and save
Friends who had ended in distress
And even strangers nonetheless,
For he in battles with vile beasts
Of the caves from the dark mists
Or with dragons from the plain
Not that easy to be slain
He used to fight with confidence,
Jumping to his friends' defense.
He gave always good advice,
Disregarding shape or size,
To cats, foxes, bears, mice.

If he was in such good form,
And good deeds he could perform,
Well, his pluck and grit were due
To the carrots which he grew,
For the carrot juice is good,
That he knew and understood,
It has vitamins and such,

Helping *strength* and muscles much.
Kung-fu, karate or such good play
Were a doddle, so to say,
And Chuck Norris, though a friend,
Was quite simply at wit's end.
If he fought Hoppity-Hop,
He could never come *out* top.

3

Hop had cottage in a glade,
Where he dug up the soil with a spade
A small garden full of flowers,
Lots of carrots giving powers.

And the forest in its length
Was inhabited by friends.
Our Hop, he liked them all,
Old and young, or big and small.

4

With his fur and tail so ruddy,
He was certainly a buddy,
The small squirrel called Nutkin.
Since old times a friend has been.

And the beaver, master joiner,
Built the cottage on the corner.

One day Hop did meet the mole
And addressed the friendly soul:
"Listen, pal, my dear mole,
Spending time in a dark hole,
You eat bugs and little maggots.
Don't you want to try my carrots?
They are sweet and packed with goodness
And can cure even blindness.
Yes my friend, take this from me
And you'll soon begin to see.
Carrots can resolve your plight
And restore your lost eyesight.
Anybody can tell you:
Carrots? They are good to chew!"

To the hedgehog he spoke thus:
"Seems to me you're a sourpuss!
Why be grouchy and bad-tempered,
Surly, testy, and ill-mannered?
Can't you be a tad more willing?
Let today be a beginning!
You're a good chap, I can tell,
Just be friendly and all's well."

Hoppy kept the wolf at bay
For the rogue had snatched away
Some fat ewes from fold and pen
Which he raided now and then
Since Hop-Hop gave him a warning
After meat he has been yearning,
Nasty tricks he won't perform
Any way, in shape, or form.

The whole pack is feeding on
Juicy carrots one-by-one.
But a stash of meaty pie
Escaped bunny's alert eye
In case Hop had gone away,
Their promise they'd betray.
For there is a well-known law,
Which the bunny would ignore:
Carrots, turnips, leeks or such
Wolves will never ever touch.

The sly fox, what can I say?
Tried, of course, to have his way
He would raid the nearby wood
For a scrap of tasty food.
Recently he's done his best
To chew carrots for a test.
But despite his efforts, true,
He'd still pinch a fish or two.
It has been known since long ago

Bear and fox had some agro:
The bear had lost its mighty tail
Which the fox schemed to curtail.
Hop approached the tailless bear
And explained it was unfair
To bear the fox an endless grudge
And each other to misjudge,
For the bear was good and kind
And the fox had changed his mind.

Soon the world started to speak
As the news began to leak
About the happy motley crew
Which the tale does now pursue
Living nice and peacefully
Always chewing merrily
Carrot, berry, hazelnut,
Never ever getting fat.

There was a row or two,
But with no further ado,
For Hop knew how to appease
Everybody with great ease.

Good-for-nothings – he'd give chase
Straight away to foreign space,
But he would never kick or whack
Those whom others don't attack,
Who were nice and stayed at home,
Not wanting to stray or roam.

For a while peace reigned all over,
Old and young lived all in clover,
But one day, out of the blue,
When Hop had digging to do,
On a fair summer's day
When you'd go outside and play,
Peace was suddenly disturbed
And a sobbing voice was heard:
"Help me", a deer said in tears,
"For I'm overwhelmed with fears,
A lion snatched my baby fawn
While he was playing on the lawn,
My darling baby, good and sweet,
The lion wants to kill and eat."
"A lion here, in our land?
Things like this are quite unplanned,
There is no zoo around here
And Africa is nowhere near,
How strange, he thought, I must confess
I've never seen such cheekiness.

Lions will be lions, there's no doubt,
But they're not allowed to flout,
A rule which our wolves obey
And they choose to stay away
From sprightly lambs and fawns and such,
Leave them alone, thanks very much!
Can't the lions do the same,
Become gentle, good, and tame?
But enough, it's time to fight
For my friends' unhappy plight!"
A carrot chewing, nice and sweet,
He set off the beast to meet.

In a jiffy he was there
And thus spoke the plucky hare:
"To you good day
Though I must say
Make haste to leave,
Else I believe
You'll have to grieve!
From baby fawn you'll keep away
Go home, I don't accept delay!"

"How dare you? the lion roared,
"Or do you think I am now bored
Or scared of a worthless hare
About whom I would not care?"
"A worthless hare, well, maybe,
But I'm forcing you to flee.
There's a book which speaks of those
Who guarding their land they chose,
They can an evil foe defeat
And overcome to a retreat.

Don't think that this is just a joke
I'm keeping you off my folk.
You may be a horrendous beast,
But beware you'll soon be fleeced
You have not been behaving, so,
I swear to strike you in a mo".
The lion's luck soon became grim,
As Hop knocked the pluck out of him
He used a quick karate trick
Hitting his muzzle with a kick
And the fawn which had been seized
Was in this way at once released.

The lion thought he'd better flee
As far from here that could be,
Go away another land
With animals docile and bland,
As far as possible from rabbits,
Karate and such other habits.
Hoppity had a word to say
After the terrible affray:
"Listen, you lion, my old chum,
I could have left you deaf and dumb
And your mighty bushy tail
Could have turned teeny and frail.

How could you, lion, serious beast,
To stoop so low, to say the least?
So, if you wish to go home free,
You'll have to promise this to me:
You will relinquish meat and bones
And try my carrots or some scones,
Or even turnips and fresh cabbage
And some fruit juice as beverage.
Redeem yourself, follow the trend,
And in this way you'll be my friend,
I suggest you: eat some veg,
Have one just now and sign a pledge.
I don't eat meat, but look at you,
So easily I beat you blue!
I have punched you without fear
Both in the face and in the rear.
Do try some carrots, bite and chew,
And no one will be quite like you,
Both confident and healthier
And braver, stronger, chirpier".

But then one night when no one knew
The beast vanished without adieu.

In another tale we hear
How a dragon spreading fear
Came to Hop's enchanted land
On a vile predator errand.
Being huge, fright he'd inspire,
Belching devastating fire.
And what claws and mighty wings!
One had never seen such things.
Hop himself had never met
Such a beast and such a threat.

He was roaring deafening
And his smell was quite appalling
Of brimstone, smoke, pus and decay,
His stench could kill you right away.
He had demanded every day
They would serve him on a tray
Three young cubs with tender meat
Which he liked to sniff and eat.
Else the punishment was dire:
Everything would be afire,
For his nostrils were a furnace,
Dreadful, terrifying menace.

So the owl in all its wisdom
Rallied through animal kingdom
And addressed both young and old:
"Come to fight, be brave and bold,
Friends it's time to take up arms,
Else the dragon us all harms."
"Owl, we know, you got it right,
But Hop is the one to fight!"
Then the beasts spoke to the hare:
"Kill the dragon in his lair!"
"I'd be mad to heed their will"
But as he pondered standing still,
He wondered how to use a trick
To smack the dragon to the quick.
And if he were to fail this time,
At least he tried to foil a crime.
Meanwhile the ugly, nasty beast.
Was expecting his large feast,
Lying down and full of anger,
Keen like mad to sate his hunger

And indeed he was so starved
That he'd have killed for tasty lard
But our Hop was not afraid
The scornful dragon to upbraid:
"Are you pitiless and haughty?
Well, I think, you are just naughty.
You may bellow, howl, or frown,
But for me you're just a clown.
A dragon with a head or two
Is no big deal, nothing new.
But if you were a dinosaur
You'd still be asked to leave our shore.
You don't belong here, mark this well,
If you don't leave, we'll give you hell.
Actually you're a lizard
Swept away by a strong blizzard,
A crocodile if you so wish
Ugly, mean, and devilish.

Well, about your fine looks,
They are silly in my books.
The bunny hoped the beast to rile
Mocking him with nasty guile,
Thought that if he vexed the beast,
His throat flames will be decreased.
But instead Hop's plan went wrong
And it did not take too long
For the dragon to belch fire
In a fit of dreadful ire.
So it did not seem alright
To entice the beast to fight.

24

"Now I think I'll mock no more
It can't be an easy war.
Better dash across the field
Till the beast would finally yield."
Quick the bunny squatted low
By some strawberries below
Dragons often are allergic
And as such much less choleric,
And if strawberries they sniff,
They can fly off in a tiff,
The bunny knew that dragons suffer
From such lurgies and other matter
And if he'd ever berries smell
His big nose would run and swell.

So at once, as stung by bees,
He began to cough and sneeze
From his eyes and down his cheek
Tears rolled and he felt meek,
Dowsing his relentless fire
Taming his horrendous ire.

Now the dragon lost his pluck,
Nonetheless he came unstuck.
So, having lost his blazing furnace,
He still tried Hoppity to menace:
"With a spin and triple flip
I shall give you awful gip
You've no time to say hello
And I strike you with a blow"

"Ha, Hoppity said thereafter
Howling loud with scornful laughter,
Your grandparents told you stories
Dealing with fights and glories,
Now you think you're deft and sly,
So that I'll begin to cry?"

26

"We have no granddads and grannies
And are never young, like bunnies."
"So you've always been this tall
Never been lovely and small?
No one ever spoilt you silly?
Everything was sad and chilly?
Have you never had some treats,
Toys and cakes, balloons, or sweets?
My gran often used to make
My good all-time carrot cake
And granddad taught me to fight
Like a bold and skillful knight."

"As I've never had a granny
All was awry and uncanny"
And the dragon full of fears,
Burst into regretful tears.
With his runny nose he sobbed
"All my life I killed and robbed.
Now I am a laughing stock
You are right to scorn and mock.

Don't you see, I fume no more,
As I did in days of yore.
What am I to make of this?
I have lost my joy and bliss.
All my body's full of zits,
Nasty blisters, ugly pits,
For instead of scales of gold,
My skin's wrinkly and old."

28

"O, you poor, wretched soul,
How could I you now console,
Would you like a carrot, say,
You'll feel happy straight away.
If you take one, you will see
How delighted you will be.
Nasty allergies they cure
I know this, you can be sure.

You will feel refreshed and glad,
Quite a happy, healthy lad.
If you munch just veg and fruit
You'll feel charming and astute.
If you do so, in the end,
I'll consider you my friend.

Now I'll give you some advice:
If you want to strike as nice,
Please, take showers every day,
Keep the awful smell at bay".
Hop has told him very sweetly,
In a friendly way, discreetly.
Taught him his teeth to brush
The microbes from his mouth to flush.
So the beast liked the advice
And became both clean and nice.

One day news spread far and quick
That an ogre, through a trick
Had arranged to lay a snare
To kidnap a damsel hare.
He had taken her from home,
Where good creatures live and roam,
Then he locked her up in jail
Where her fate she would bewail.
She was now living in fear,
Far from home, the wretched dear.
For she'd guessed his evil plot:
Marry her right on the spot.

But it didn't take too long:
Hop could clear all the wrong.
He had heard of such mean monsters
Which are ugly, witless, bonkers,
Rude and churlish, greedy-guts,
Eating thousands of doughnuts,
Although boastful, mean and dullards,
They are foolish, simple cowards.

So Hop went straight to the castle,
Ate a carrot to build muscle
And he knocked loud at the gate,
Even though it was quite late.
"Who is there, are you mad?"
Yelled the ogre from his pad.
"It is I, the wizard, Hop,
At your place having a stop.
I've an ogre now with me
Come down here and you'll see"
"Ogre? We exist no more
As we were in times of yore.

I'm the last and want to marry
A damsel-rabbit as a fairy
We'll have baby-ogres plenty,
Maybe fifteen, even twenty.
A female-rabbit easily can
Give me children, a whole clan,
Cute and nice, and sweet and small,
Looking pretty like a doll".

"Your lot are gone, the bunny said,
I have eaten them on bread.
One is left from your sort,
But his life will be cut short
Ogre was but with my wand,
Now it's carrot in my hand.

How I did it? With my magic.
Now his destiny is tragic
I'll have him as my good lunch,
For I like carrots to crunch.
And Hop-Hop, taking a bite,
From the carrot sweet and light,
Said. "The same happens to you,
For you'll be a carrot too,
Cos' you see, I am still starving,
And your turn is soon arriving.

I have eaten lots like you,
As a piece of cake to chew"
And Hop took another bite
From his carrot with delight.

"O, please Hop, please, be so kind,
I would like to speak my mind,
Stop the magic, I am rich,
I have gold and jewels which,
If you'll have mercy on me,
Everything would yours be"
Said the monster on his knee.

"I want you to leave just now,
Otherwise we'll have a row,
You will be terribly beaten,
Turned into a carrot, eaten,
So the ogres will no more
Stroll this fair and lovely shore.
Ogres, dragons we don't want,
Nor mean lions us to haunt.
We are fed up with you all
We want peace. Enough with brawl,
Friendship's good for our land,
Strife and feud we cannot stand
We don't want scoundrels like you,
Ogres, lions, dragons shoo!".

"I am off, I'm going now,
Shan't come back, this is a vow.
I am off, I'll leave this tract,
For I want to be intact".
Saying that the ogre left.
"Nobody will feel bereft"

Said the bunny, running fast
To release the girl at last.
Hop had not seen her before,
But had heard good words galore
When on her he clapped his eyes,
Felt inside him butterflies.

She was beautiful and funny,
Sweeter than the sweetest honey.
Looking at her pretty face,
He admired her charming grace.
She could even a model be,
That good-looking, fair was she.

As for her, one word to add:
She was now relieved and glad.
And aside from all above,
She fell instantly in love.
Their wedding was so funny
As it suits a gallant bunny.
They had ice-cold carrot juice
And green lettuces for mousse.

Then they danced the night away
Everything was like a play.
And the hedgehog known as sour,
Having on his breast a flower,
Was as glad as everyone
And he had a lot of fun.

Hop chose me as his best man
And he told me, "If you can,
Go to your grandchildren now
And tell them the story how
I could find a pretty wife
And for all a peaceful life.

Well, you were best man to me,
Soon godfather you will be"

Printed in the United States
By Bookmasters